The Evil Plan

Isaac Nkrumah Darko

Published by Revival Waves of Glory Books & Publishing

PO Box 596| Litchfield, Illinois 62056 USA

www.revivalwavesofgloryministries.com

Revival Waves of Glory Books & Publishing is committed to excellence in the publishing industry.

Book design Copyright © 2017 by Revival Waves of Glory Books & Publishing. All rights reserved.

Published in the United States of America

ISBN: 978-1-68411-478-8

"The word of God is an antidote for all human problems, not only in this world but also the world to come."

— Isaac Nkrumah Darko

Contents

Chapter One

A s the early morning sun shed its rays on a Tuesday in Binso, the birds chirped as they soared in the air and Frimpong's wife, Araba, performed her household chores with much enthusiasm by singing sweet melodies to cheer her on. At eleven o'clock, when people had crowded in the market to undertake commercial transactions, Araba made up her mind to go to the market.

"Sweetheart, it is getting late in the morning and I must go to the market to buy food items," she said.

"How much will you need?" Frimpong asked.

"Thirty Ghana cedis."

"Wait for me. I'll be back very soon." Frimpong rushed to the adjacent room and picked up a wallet from a drawer. When he opened it, there was an amount of twenty-five Ghana cedis in it. "I've only twenty-five Ghana cedis in my wallet. Take it and manage it," he said when he came back to Araba.

"Try to add the remaining five Ghana cedis to it because twenty-five Ghana cedis can't buy the food items."

"Hmmm!" Frimpong sighed. "I've no money left. You must cut down the expenses."

"If that's the situation, then I'll try to manage it like that."

"You're a good wife who easily understands issues."

Araba hurried to the room to change her dress and took a basket and ambled to a cold store at the market. "Do you have meat in there?" she asked.

"Yes," the saleswoman said.

"What type of meat?"

"That of a turkey."

"How much do you sell them for?"

"Some are worth five Ghana cedis and others are worth ten and fifteen Ghana cedis."

"Give me what I can get for five Ghana cedis."

The saleswoman put the meat in a bag and gave it to Araba when she had paid for it. Being at the mercy of the scorching sun, her body emitted sweat, so she took a white handkerchief from her pocket to mop the sweat and galloped to a restaurant to buy food to eat.

"Give me a meal costing five Ghana cedis," she told the waitress who served her the food. But after eating, when Araba unzipped her purse to get the money to pay for the food, there was no money in it. "Eh! Where is my money? I can't find it."

"Have you come here to dupe me?" asked the waitress.

"No." Araba pleaded with her to exercise patience.

"Then why didn't you have money when you come in? Did you forget it?"

"No." Araba scratched the back of her neck. "I had money."

"And, where is it?"

"It's missing."

The waitress swayed on her feet. "So how do you pay for the food?"

"Let me go home and come back."

"It's not done."

Araba begged the waitress. "Consider my situation."

"If I allow you to leave and my manager learns about it, he'll bring me to a book. Call your relative on the phone to bring you some money."

Not knowing what more to say, Araba called Frimpong on the phone. "Sweetheart, I'm at a restaurant."

"Have you gone to the market to buy the items?" Frimpong asked.

"Yes, but I haven't bought all the items."

"Then you must hurry up to buy them."

"The money is missing and I want you to bring me some more money."

"Don't you know that the money I gave to you was all the money I had?" Frimpong's voice thundered. "If the money is missing, then come home and let us starve. I can't come."

"Why can't you come?"

Frimpong lost his temper. "Do you want me to come and carry you on my back to the house?"

Araba lowered her voice. "I've been detained in the restaurant for being unable to pay for the food I have ordered and eaten."

"If the money is missing, why would you go to order food to eat at a restaurant?"

"I didn't know the money was missing until I had ordered the food and eaten it."

"So, what do you want me to do since I don't have money?"

"Try to find some and bring it to me."

"Then wait for me for a while. I'm going to borrow money from my younger brother. I'll come there if he gives it to me."

"All right. You must hurry up."

When Frimpong rushed to his brother's house to look for him, he was nowhere to be found. Eager to find him, he phoned him. "Hello, Boafo! Where are you?"

"I'm at the farm."

"I'm at your house for an urgent issue."

"Then wait for me. I'm getting prepared to come home," Boafo said.

"I can't wait for you to come from the farm because the matter is too urgent."

"Has something serious happened?"

"I just need some money urgently."

"Is it a big amount of money?"

Frimpong placed his left palm on his waist while making the phone call. "I need thirty Ghana cedis."

Boafo empathized with him and was eager to help him. "Go to Annan to collect thirty Ghana cedis."

"Call him on the phone to notify him that you've asked me to collect thirty Ghana cedis from him," Frimpong said.

Boafo stood under a mango tree to call Annan on the phone. "Hello Annan, I'm at the farm and there is something urgent at the house, so give thirty Ghana cedis to my brother, Frimpong."

"All right. But where is Frimpong?"

"He is at my house and he'll be coming to you very soon."

When Frimpong went for the money, he galloped to the restaurant to pay for Araba's food. "I've brought the money. Go and call the waitress to come," he told Araba.

Araba stood up from her chair, stretched herself and rushed to call the waitress. "Madam, my husband has come to pay the money."

"Tell him to wait. I'll be there in a few minutes."

"My darling, wait for the waitress for a while. She is attending to some customers and she'll come very soon," Araba said when she came back to Frimpong.

As they were chatting, the waitress came. "You've done well to bring the money yourself. I thought you would send a boy to bring it."

Frimpong smiled. "It is not a difficult task to bring the money myself. I'm also hungry. Give me food to enjoy so that I pay it in addition to that of my wife?"

"What food do you prefer?" the waitress asked.

"Any affordable food."

"All the meals on the menu are affordable." The waitress showed him the menu.

"Then I'll always come here to eat."

"That's what we expect of our customers."

"Give me rice and stew."

"How much?" asked the waitress.

"The same amount as that of my wife."

"Five Ghana cedis?"

"Exactly." Frimpong jostled in his chair.

In haste, the waitress brought the food to him. But when he tried to thrust his right hand into his back pocket for money to pay for the food, a customer called the waitress and she hurried to attend to him. So, for the meantime, Frimpong didn't take the money from his pocket and enjoyed the food.

After he had finished eating the food, the waitress came for the money.

"I must take a drink to quench my appetite, so bring me a bottle of malt," he said.

The waitress hurried to bring it to him and uncorked it for him and while he took a sip of it, she stretched out her right hand for the money. "Give me the money."

"What's the total cost?" Frimpong asked.

"Your food and that of your wife cost ten Ghana cedis and the drink is four Ghana cedis, so you'll give me fourteen Ghana cedis," the waitress explained.

When Frimpong inserted his hand in his pocket for the money to pay for the food, there was no money in it. "Where is the money? I can't find it." His face contorted as he was surprised.

"What you and your wife are doing seems strange! How can you and your wife's money get lost after eating in the restaurant?"

"Please, exercise patience. We'll pay the money." Frimpong unbuttoned his shirt and unbuckled his belt to search for the money.

"So, what should I do, now that you don't have any money to pay for the food?"

Frimpong pleaded with her. "Calm down and give us more time to put things in order."

The waitress frowned. "How long should I exercise patience?"

Because he was worried and didn't understand how the money got missing, Frimpong walked away from the restaurant, leaving Araba behind. He diligently looked for the money as he ambled along the path. Not being careful, he hit his foot against a stone on the path and blood oozed from the wound. "Ah! I've hurt my foot!" He stooped down to massage it to assuage the pain. "Why these problems? I've hurt my foot because of small money."

As he lamented, a ten-year-old boy passed by him and he beckoned to him. "Boy! Come here."

The boy hurried to him. "Is there anything I can do for you?"

"Not really but did you find any money along the path?"

"No." The boy shook the head. "I met two boys who told me they had found some money. They asked me whether I had lost my money."

"Where are they?"

"They're on the way to the town. You can catch up with them."

"Do you know their names?"

"Yes." The boy nodded.

"Then tell me their names."

"The older one is Kobina and the younger one is Donkor."

"I may forget their names, so I have to write them." Frimpong moved closer to the boy. "Do you have a pen and a sheet of paper on you?"

"No. But look ahead. There's a school girl coming. You can ask her."

Frimpong limped on his hurt foot to meet the school girl. "Give me a pen and a sheet of paper."

The school girl opened her school bag and took out a pen and a sheet of paper for him, but he declined them. "Don't give them to me yet. Write some names on the paper for me."

"What are the names?" asked the school girl.

"Kobina and Donkor."

The girl school wrote the names on the paper and gave it to Frimpong who limped to town and moved from individual to individual, asking for the boys. "Young man, do you know Kobina and Donkor?"

"I live in the same vicinity with them," the young man said.

"Have you seen them around?"

"I saw them playing a football match."

"Where?"

"At the CP Park."

Chapter Two

Relieved of his worries, Frimpong limped to the CP Park to look for the boys who were playing football in the park. He approached five spectators who had gathered watching the match. These spectators, thrilled by the performance of the players, were singing and clapping to cheer them on. One of the players dribbled the ball and kicked it to score a goal and the goalkeeper tossed himself to catch it, but to no avail.

"Goal, go-o-o-al! Donkor has scored the goal." Some of the players jubilated and carried him shoulder-high.

Frimpong showed the names on the paper to the spectators. "I'm looking for these boys."

"Kobina and Donkor are among the players. Donkor is the one who just scored the goal," the spectators said.

"Call them for me!"

One of the spectators went to the captain of the winning team and whispered into his ear. "Somebody is looking for Kobina and Donkor."

The captain shouted to call Kobina and Donkor and they rushed to him. "Here we are."

The captain turned back and stretched out his right hand towards the pole. "The fair man, standing behind the pole is looking for you."

"Who is he?" they asked.

"I don't know," said the captain.

Kobina and Donkor, who were eager to hear what Frimpong had for them, ran to him. "Here we are. The captain says you need us."

"My money has gotten lost along the path, leading to the Pleasure Restaurant and a boy, whom I met on the path, says you found money along the path."

"How much?" asked Donkor.

"Thirty Ghana cedis."

"Sorry. We found thirty Ghana cedis along the path, but you didn't come early for the money."

"Why?"

Donkor stretched out the right hand towards the ball in the center of the park. "We used it to buy the football that we're playing with in the park."

"I'm doomed." Frimpong was dejected and went home to meet his brother, Boafo, who had come from the farm and was reclining in a chair, taking a sip of coffee.

"The money has been lost," he said.

"How did it get lost?"

"I can't even explain it." Frimpong narrated the incident to Boafo.

"So how do you pay for the meals?" Boafo asked.

"That's why I've come to you again to tell your debtor whether he can still get some money for me."

Boafo pulled up his legs in the chair. "After he had given the money to you, he called me on the phone to make me aware of it and told me the money was all that he had on him. Why don't you see Adjoa whether she can lend you some money?"

"My wife will be the right person to do so, since she is her friend."

"Then why don't you let her do so?"

"She is at the restaurant."

"Doing what?"

"She has been detained there until we pay for the meal."

Boafo hit his right hand on a table. "Wha-a-at! It's unheard of to detain someone in a restaurant for being unable to pay the cost of a meal. This is unlawful."

Frimpong placed the left hand on the arm of his chair. "Let's not bother about legalities. After all, we owe them and they may have a cause to do that."

"You must do something about it. Why should your wife be detained at the restaurant?"

"I'll let my wife go to Adjoa to borrow some money."

"But will they allow your wife to leave the restaurant since you haven't pay for the meals?"

"No. But I'll go and replace her there so that she can go for the money."

After the conversation with his brother, Frimpong dashed to the restaurant in dejection.

"Sweetheart, have you gotten the money?" Araba asked.

"No." Frimpong shook the right hand. "My brother doesn't have any money."

"Then why have you come? Do you want me to be detained here all day?"

"I've come to replace you so that you can go to your friend, Adjoa, to borrow the money."

"I owe her, so it's not good to borrow money from her again."

"It doesn't matter. You can explain the situation to her and she'll empathize with us and lend us some money."

"Okay." The corners of Araba's mouth turned up. "I'll go and try."

While they were talking, the waitress came over and demanded the money. She stared at Frimpong. "Have you brought the money?"

"Erm, no."

The waitress wrinkled her face. "Why are you refusing to pay for the food you have eaten? Do you want me to call the security officers to harass you?"

"Please, don't do that," Araba said. "We'll pay the money."

"When?"

"Today."

"At what time?"

Araba tugged at her earlobe. "Erm, today."

The waitress lost her temper. "At what time of the day? Do you want me to notify the management of your unwillingness to pay for the food so that they deal with you harshly?"

Araba begged her. "Give us a little more time to make payment."

"Didn't your husband bring the money?"

Frimpong cut in. "I haven't brought the money. I've come to let my wife go for the money from someone."

"I can't allow both of you to go while you haven't paid for the meals. What if I don't see you again?"

"Only my wife will go and I'll stay here," Frimpong said.

"Are you sure your wife can get the money when she goes?" asked the waitress.

"Precisely."

"Then let her go."

Araba was not happy with what was happening so she dashed to the house to look for Adjoa to borrow the money. "Adjoa, can you lend me twenty Ghana cedis to enable me to solve an issue at stake?"

"Is it a good or bad issue?" Adjoa took money from her purse and gave it to her.

On collecting the money, Araba counted it to confirm whether it is twenty Ghana cedis. "It's not twenty Ghana cedis."

"How much is it?" Adjoa asked.

"Fifteen Ghana cedis. But it can still solve the issue."

"Let me add the remaining five Ghana cedis to it." Adjoa rushed to another room and opened a bag to take five Ghana cedis to Araba.

"Thank you." Araba counted the money again. "All right. I'll bring it back to you next week."

"Don't bring it. I've given it to you."

"Thanks. You've surprised me."

Relieved of her worries, Araba walked back to the restaurant, but when she was crossing a road, a taxi knocked her down and she was injured. Blood oozed from her nose and she lay breathless on the road.

Two men, who first saw her, rushed her to a hospital. "This is tragic. Araba is dead," they said when they carried her shoulder-high to the nearby hospital.

While Frimpong was waiting for her to bring the money, a girl ran to tell him that she was dead. "Your wife is dead!" Tears trickled down the girl's cheeks.

"Wha-a-a-at! I don't believe it. What happened?" Frimpong was shocked and his face turned gloomy.

"A taxi knocked her down when she was crossing the road."

Frimpong shivered. "I'm doomed. Why should my wife die prematurely?" He started weeping and his eyes turned red as sadness gripped him and when he could not control his emotions, he fell to the ground.

Sensing danger for him, the girl and one of the security men conveyed him to a hospital. His family members and friends trooped to the hospital to see him. The doctors had diagnosed him and were treating him. They had taken his temperature and pulse and given him injections.

"Don't be paranoid. Frimpong will be well." The doctors assured the family members who were in a panic and thought that he would die. After two hours, Frimpong became well and asked of his wife.

"Where is my wife? Has she died? I want to see her."

"Don't worry. She'll be well," the family members said.

The doctors prescribed other medications for him and discharged him. "Take this form to the pharmacist to collect the drugs and come next week for a review."

When Frimpong presented the form to the pharmacist, he ordered him to sit in a queue to wait for him awhile. Frimpong folded his arms and gnashed his teeth, thinking about the wife.

"Frimpong," the pharmacist called him.

"Yes sir."

"Come for your drugs."

Frimpong stood in haste and went for the drugs and while the pharmacist explained the dosage of the drugs to him, he nodded.

When he went home, news had spread in the vicinity that Araba had not died. She had been unconscious but some of the people reported that she was dead. Such news enraptured him and dissipated his worries. He leaped amid throwing his hands to demonstrate his happiness and renewed emotional strength. "I'm more than happy to hear that my wife is not dead and that what I heard was misinformation. Such misinformation could have sent me to the grave had it not been for the timely intervention of doctors."

Three days later, Araba was discharged from the hospital and some people sympathized with her. She narrated what had led to her accident to the sympathizers who encouraged her that things would change for good and her financial situation would improve.

"I was detained at the restaurant for hours because of just five Ghana cedis. What a disgrace?" She grieved over the situation.

"It is not a disgrace. Things will change for good." The sympathizers consoled her. "But have you paid for the meal?"

"No."

"Then, we'll go and pay it tomorrow," said the sympathizers.

While the conversation was going on, the waitress, who had heard that Araba and Frimpong had been discharged from the hospital, came there.

"Oh sorry. I didn't know such a terrible thing could happen to you. All the workers of the restaurant are remorseful about what ensued between us,"' the waitress mumbled.

"Are you the waitress?" asked Araba's friend.

"Yes."

"Tomorrow morning, I'll come and pay the money," the friend said.

"It is needless to pay it. Use it to buy something for her."

Araba belched and coughed.

"Araba, is there anything you want to tell me?" asked the waitress.

"No. Too many worries make me belch and cough."

"Get rid of your worries because there're better things ahead," the waitress said and left the place.

Chapter Three

Two days after the incident, a farmer named Munko rushed to Frimpong early in the morning to collect his money. Frimpong had bought food items on credit from him for the past three weeks but hadn't paid it. Munko banged on the door of the house.

"Who is it?" Frimpong shouted.

Munko didn't respond, but continued to bang on the door until Frimpong came to open it.

"Is it you? Why didn't you respond?"

"I'm here to collect my money."

"It is too early, so go and come back." Frimpong stretched himself and yawned.

Munko's countenance fell. "Come back at what time?"

"At nine o'clock."

"I can't go and come again. I'll wait until nine o'clock. You've been playing tricks on me."

"It's not good to wait here till nine o'clock."

"Why?" Munko raised his palms.

"It won't speak well of me to let you sit here till nine o'clock before I pay the money."

"Then pay it now if you've got the money here."

Frimpong cleared the throat. "I don't have the money now."

"So how can you pay it at nine o'clock?" Munko's eyes widened. "Do you want to play tricks on me again?"

"By that time, I may have gotten the money," Frimpong said.

"From where?"

"From my friends."

Munko gazed at his face. "You see! You want to trick me to go away. But I won't go till you pay me the money!"

During the time Frimpong and Munko were exchanging words, a woman, Afia, came there for the money Frimpong owed her. "Today, I won't go until you pay my money to me."

"You're making too much noise. Stop it," Frimpong yelled.

Afia rocked on her feet. "If you don't want noise, then pay my money to me."

"What will the noise do?"

"If it won't do anything, then don't ask me to stop making it."

"Do you want to make me lose my temper and force you out of my house?"

"You can do whatever you like. I don't care." Afia shook her body. "How can you buy a bag of rice on credit, without trying to pay for it? Do you want me to go bankrupt for my business to collapse?"

"Give me more time to pay it. I'm not the only debtor in the world."

"Want more time again? It won't be possible." Afia thrust her right hand into Frimpong's back pocket for money, but he resisted her by struggling with her.

"This is not the right way to collect your money from me." Frimpong gripped her to force her out of the house.

As the dispute erupted between them, Munko departed from the house. "I'm going home, but I'll come back tomorrow for my money."

"It will be best if you come next week," said Frimpong.

"Next week? Why?" Munko squared his shoulders. "That means you don't want to pay me the money."

"That is not the issue."

"But why are you asking me to come next week?"

"For the sake of convenience."

"No problem." Munko pointed out the forefinger at him to warn him. "I'll come next week, but should you fail to pay the money, I'll be hostile to you."

As soon as Munko had left the house, Afia continued to engage Frimpong in a dispute, explaining that she would not leave the house until he paid the money to her. And while Frimpong walked to his hall, she followed him, hurling insults at him. "You're irresponsible. Give me my money."

"Keep quiet and let me have peace of mind. Go away from my hall," Frimpong yelled, rolling his eyes.

"I won't go. I'll be in your house till you pay my money to me."

"I don't care, but you'll see what my wife will come and do to you."

"Your wife can't do anything to me. I will fight her."

As Frimpong was sitting on a sofa in the hall while Afia exchanged words with him, he cupped his chin and began to think. *How am I going to get money to pay my debts? I can't bear embarrassments anymore. I need to find a solution to my financial problems.*

"Mr. Frimpong, why are you stingy and unwilling to pay my money?" Afia scoffed at him.

"How many times do you want me to tell you that I don't have any money? Go and come next week."

"I won't go till you give me the money. I'll sleep here if you don't pay the money."

"I don't mind whether you sleep here."

"Do you think I'm joking?" Afia took clothes and spread them on the floor and lay supine on them, moving her legs back and forth. "I'm sleeping here to prove to you that I don't joke with my words."

Frimpong stared at her. "Afia, why are you behaving like this? I thought you were joking. It is not normal to sleep in my hall because I owe you."

Frimpong, enraged by her behavior, approached her but as he stooped down to hold her hands to force her out of the hall, he slipped and fell on her and unintentionally got hold of her breast. Such a bizarre incident erupted lustful waves into their bodies and they looked into each other's eyes.

"Sheiee! What a loving touch?" Afia licked her lips.

"Sorry." Frimpong removed the hand on her breast. "This is an unintentional touch."

Afia, who was interested in Frimpong, wriggled her body and put her hands around him. "You're lovable. I've cancelled your debts," she said and kissed him while he also kissed her.

"Your kisses are lovely," Frimpong said.

Afia giggled. "Yours too."

"Then let me give you more."

Afia resisted his kiss. "Wait. Here is an open place. We can easily be seen."

"Then let's go to the bedroom."

"Is your wife not around?"

"Yes."

"Where is she?"

"She woke up early and left for the market. She'll come back in the evening."

"Then we can enjoy ourselves."

Being under the spell of infatuation, Frimpong unbuttoned his shirt to remove it and squatted. "Come and let me carry you on my back to the bedroom because you're precious and exquisite."

Afia shook her buttocks in the view of Frimpong. "It is nice for you to carry me on your back. But you should stoop down for me to get on your back instead of squatting."

Without hesitation, Frimpong stood upright, stretched himself and then stooped down. "Come and get on my back."

Afia, being hungry for love making, rested her body on Frimpong's back and he carried her to the bedroom.

Chapter Four

One afternoon, a boy asked Ankra for money. Ankra was a thirty-year-old rich man in Binso, but how he had obtained his riches had become a bone of contention among the people. Some claimed that he had obtained his riches through dubious means while others debunked the claim as an attempt to defame him. He owned a fleet of cars of different models and made a show of his riches in public places and meetings. As a result, the townspeople nicknamed him Showman and the name stuck.

Whenever someone hailed him by calling him Showman, he raised his hand in response and gave the person money. This attitude on his part made him popular in the town.

"Showman!" a boy shouted.

"Yeah. Come for money." He raised his hand. The boy rushed for the money and smiled and ran home, shouting that Showman had given him money.

A young woman, Mintaah, who heard him approached him and asked of Showman's whereabouts.

"Where is Showman?" Mintaah asked.

"He is in the drinking bar." The boy pointed out his right hand towards the drinking bar.

"I'm also going for my share of money." Mintaah hurried to the drinking bar to look for Showman. On reaching there, some people had surrounded him and were hailing him. While they called him Showman, he gave them money. Mintaah stood before him and stretched out her right hand for money. "Showman, give me my share of the money." But when Showman saw her, he asked her to sit in a chair to wait for him and ordered the people whom he had not yet given money to go away and come next time, explaining that the money on him was getting low.

Some of the people grumbled as they left the place. "I'm not lucky. I didn't get my share of the money from Showman. Anytime he gives out money, I don't get any. Why?" A girl mumbled.

Showman went to sit in a chair in front of that of Mintaah and they faced each other.

"It's a pleasure to meet you here?" he said.

Mintaah smiled. "That's good."

"Wonderful! You've a musical voice and I hope you're a musician or singer."

"Yeah." Mintaah nodded.

"Oh nice. Beautiful women normally have a musical voice."

"Am I beautiful?" Mintaah's face radiated with joy.

"Don't you know it yourself?"

"I don't."

"You can't know it because sugar cannot boast of its sweetness. It is the eater who can do so. I'm the eater and you're the sugar. Therefore, what I say is the truth."

"Wow! You're cheerful." Mintaah's pupils dilated.

Showman adjusted his tie. "May I know who you are?"

"I'm Mintaah and I live in the Zonal Estate."

"I see. I'll be coming to visit you there."

"That will be nice of you." Mintaah flipped her hair back. "You're always welcome."

Showman stood up. "Wait for me. I'll be back in a few minutes." He went to take money from a briefcase in his car which he had parked in front of the drinking bar. "I'm back." As he talked with Mintaah, he held the collar of her dress. "There's an ant on the collar of your dress."

"Where is it? Let me see it."

Showman caught the ant and showed it to her.

"Where did it come from?" Mintaah threw it on the floor and stamped on it to kill it.

Showman gazed into her eyes and he used his forefinger to touch the tip of her nose. "Your nose is lovely."

"I'd like to go home to do household chores," said Mintaah.

"You can go but let me do you a favor."

"What favor?"

"Give you a lift."

"From here to where I'm going is not far. I can walk."

"It matters not."

"Okay. Let's go." Mintaah followed Showman to his car.

While Showman drove the car, he talked with her.

When Mintaah alighted from the car, she waved goodbye to Showman but as she moved two steps forward, he called her. "Mintaah, come."

Mintaah turned backed to see him. "Should I come?"

"Yes. I've forgotten to give you something." Showman unzipped his wallet and took money from it. "Take this money."

Mintaah collected it. "Thank you."

"But how do I see you again?"

"I'm always available at home. You can send for me."

"Why not give me your phone number, so that I call you?"

Mintaah called out her phone numbers to Showman and he entered them on his mobile phone.

"Let me recall the numbers to make sure I've typed them correctly." But to Showman's surprise, when he dialed the numbers, it was out of coverage area. "It's not going through. Is your phone here?"

"It is off. It is on charge in the house," Mintaah said.

"Then expect my call in the evening."

On reaching home, Mintaah reclined in a chair, folded her arms and pondered, *Is Showman in love with me? He has been friendly and generous to me. What's the notion behind his attitude? Is it a platonic love or romantic love?*

Her elder brother came to her. "It's 4:30 p.m. and you must prepare food for supper," he said.

"What food should I cook?" asked Mintaah.

"What you think is good."

Mintaah got up from the chair, yawned and strolled to the kitchen to collect food items into a cooking utensil. As she chopped the vegetables into pieces, the knife cut her middle finger and blood oozed from it. She used a napkin to mop the blood and to ease the pain.

Having washed the food items, she put them in a special utensil and put it on a fire to prepare a stew. Within thirty minutes, the stew was well cooked and she cooked rice and she and her brother ate it with the stew. The brother, who enjoyed the food to the point of satiety, remarked, "Sister, the food is sumptuous and delicious."

At 8:00 p.m. while Mintaah was watching a movie which had captured her attention, her mobile phone rang repeatedly, but since she was engrossed in the movie, she didn't receive the call until the movie came to an end.

"Whose number is this? Let me call it." She put the phone up to her left ear when she had dialed the number. "Hello, I'm happy to call back. Who is this?"

"It's me, Showman."

"I've seen your missed calls and I'm calling back," said Mintaah.

"Will it be possible to see you tomorrow morning?" Showman asked.

"When?"

"Around 10:00 a.m."

"Yes. But is there any agenda?"

"A big one."

"Can you give me a hint of it?"

Showman toned down his voice. "To go shopping."

"This is a surprise to me."

"It shouldn't be a surprise. My showmanship is not limited to the giving of money."

"Tomorrow, I'll wait for you where you dropped me off."

"All right."

"Bye, bye!" Mintaah waved the hand as if she was seeing Showman and ended the conversation.

The next day, to her expectation Showman came to take her for shopping in a nearby city.

"It doesn't only take years to know someone, but also a day," Showman said, while he drove the car.

"That's true," Mintaah retorted.

Showman cleared her throat. "Erm, you've won my admiration and favor."

"Then I'm lucky."

Showman drove slowly. "But what are your marriage plans, if I may ask?"

Mintaah was reticent for a while and then spoke. "When the time comes."

"Don't you think this is the time?"

"No. I don't even have a fiancé."

"Are you sure?" Showman marveled.

"It is hard to believe, but that is the reality," Mintaah said.

"I don't believe it. How old are you?"

"Twenty-four."

Showman doubted her. "And no boyfriend? Then it will not be wrong to have one."

"It is wrong?"

"In what way? Are you not of age?"

"I am but I want a fiancé," Mintaah said.

"Are boyfriend and fiancé not the same?" asked Showman.

"They aren't."

"What's the difference?"

"A boyfriend is a woman's sexual partner who may or may not marry her, but a fiancé is a man that a woman is going to get married to. He may or may not necessarily be her sexual partner." Mintaah held her breath and mopped her face with a handkerchief. "A boyfriend is not necessarily someone a woman wants to marry, but a fiancé is."

"Today, you're teaching me romantic terms," Showman remarked.

When they had alighted from the car, they went to a shopping mall where they shopped. Showman bought different items, including pairs of sandals for her and she liked them. "The items are quality and I owe you thanks for your kind gesture." Mintaah was happy.

"Don't be surprised at what I've done. My showmanship is not limited to the giving of money. It has no bounds."

Immediately, they came out of the shopping mall and a man who knew Showman saw him and hailed him. "Showman, the best philanthropist."

He raised his right hand. "To call me Showman is to move me into action."

"Then you must act," the man said.

"To act is to ask you to come for your share of money." He took money from his wallet and gave it to the man.

"Showman!" the man yelled upon receiving it.

"Yeah." Showman raised his hand in response. "I'm the best philanthropist."

Chapter Five

As time elapsed, Mintaah often visited Showman at the house while he also visited her at her house. This strengthened their friendship and Showman continued to do good to her.

One evening, Showman invited Mintaah to his bedroom to have a special discussion with her. "To invite you to my bedroom is a sign that the message I have for you is serious," he said.

"Will it bring money?" asked Mintaah.

"You've got it. He who associates himself with a great person paves the way for his own greatness. Therefore, your association with me must pave way for your riches."

"Good. Your words are encouraging."

Showman looked at her face. "Do you want money?"

"Who, in this world, doesn't want money?" Mintaah replied.

"That's it. You're beautiful and a good marriage can make you better off and rich."

Mintaah wondered. "A good marriage? To who?"

"My friend."

"Who is your friend?"

"You'll soon know him."

"Do you intend to choose a husband for me? Have you forgotten the saying that no one teaches a child how to crack a bone?"

"I'm just making a suggestion."

"What work does your friend do?" Mintaah asked.

"He is a pastor who is rich," Showman answered.

Mintaah's face beamed. "Wow! Do I know him?"

"No. He is a pastor in a glorious chapel."

"Has he expressed an interest in me?"

Showman locked his ankles. "He has told me he wants to marry, but he has no fiancée in mind. So, I want to link you to him."

"Can you do it?"

"Why not? Don't you trust me?" I've methods to link you to him. I just need your consent."

"Does he truly have money?"

"Don't mention it. He is richer than I am and has more fame than I have."

Mintaah became interested in the conversation. "Are you sure you can get him to marry me?"

"Very easy," Showman said. "He is my childhood friend, but after graduating from college, he went to a pastoral school while I went into business and he is chalking a great success in ministry."

Mintaah fiddled with her mobile phone. "I've agreed to your suggestion, but why did you decide to choose me for him?"

"You're not only well mannered, but also beautiful so I don't want riff-raff to marry you and give you problems."

"Thanks for the good intentions you have for me."

When Mintaah left for her house after the discussion, Showman laughed and thought, *I'll use Mintaah as an instrument to bring Pastor Essel down. Pastor Essel and I have been friends since childhood and he is from a poor family and didn't even go to university after college.* He moved his palm over his face. *So now, why should he be richer than me and why should people revere and hail him more than me. I'll make people have no regard for him?*

The next day, Showman went to Pastor Essel to know how he was faring. "How are you coping with the circumstances of life?" he asked.

"By the grace of God, things are moving on smoothly," Pastor Essel said.

Showman raised his forefinger towards heaven. "Thanks be to God."

"Is your wife with you?"

"No. She has traveled. But I hope very soon, you'll also have your wife."

"Yes, but it depends on the will of God."

Showman looked heavenward and yelled, "The will of God has already been done."

Pastor Essel smiled. "Amen! I like your faith inspiring words."

"As a pastor, I know you'll marry a woman in your church."

"Of course. However, it is the will of God which will determine it."

"I know you men of God can pray to God for him to reveal your wives to you," Showman said.

The dimples on Pastor Essel's face widened as he laughed. "Even though, men of God pray to God to help them choose their wives, how God links them to their wives is the decision of God, not men. Our duty is to have unwavering faith in Him."

Showman nodded. "I've understood you. But can't God let you marry a woman who is not a Christian, so that through you she becomes a Christian?"

"That may be the decision of God. However, God doesn't do things that will contradict His word in the Bible. To do that is based on human theology, but not the theology of the Holy Spirit," Pastor Essel said, making reference to the Bible. "2 Corinthians 6:14-15 says, 'Do not be yoked together with unbelievers. For what do righteousness and wickedness have in common? Or what fellowship can light have with darkness? What harmony is there between Christ and Belial? What does a believer have in common with an unbeliever?'"

Showman agreed to his explanations. "Even though I don't have spiritual insights, I can see that your explanation is inspired of the Holy Spirit."

"That's why I've been telling you to surrender your life to God to be filled with the Holy Spirit in order to have a spiritual understanding."

Showman stroked his chin. "In fact, nowadays my Christian life has retrogressed because of my much-scheduled business activities. I must confess that I don't get time to have fellowship with God."

"This is bad. The love of money is the root of all evil but dependence on God is a key for riches. This is a secret to many people."

"So, is it evil to have billions of monies?"

"No. If something is evil, it's evil regardless of its quantity and size. But the Bible does not teach that money, whether big amount or small amount, is evil but how we acquire money and use money makes money evil." Pastor Essel paused to sneeze." So, God expects us to acquire money and use it in a godly manner. This is what the statement means."

Showman, convinced with Pastor Essel's explanation, shook hands with him and remarked, "You're an expert in interpreting the scriptures."

Pastor Essel turned the face towards heaven. "Interpretations belong to God."

Three days later, Showman called Mintaah to his house. "Three days ago, I went to my friend, the pastor and erm..."

"Did you talk to him about me?" Mintaah interrupted his speech.

"No. But I found out his marriage plans and I got to know that he still doesn't have a fiancée which implies that your chance of becoming his fiancée and then wife is greater."

"Good." Mintaah's eyelashes darted. "But why didn't you introduce me to him?"

"That is why I've summoned you here to talk matters over. One person does not go into counsel," said Showman.

"So, what are we going to do?"'

"You must start attending his church for him to take notice of you and know that you're a Christian."

"Will you go with me?"

"No."

"When should I start attending the church?"

"This Sunday. After doing this, I'll be sending you to him often and later introduce you to him," Showman said, "and I know with time, he'll admire you and fall in love with you."

Just after Mintaah had gone home, Showman lay supine in his bed and put his palm on the cheek. *Everybody in this town speaks well of Pastor Essel and holds him in high esteem. Most of the women hail him more than me even though I give money to people. I'll get the same people, who hold him in high esteem, to disregard him by using Mintaah as an instrument*, he pondered.

When Sunday arrived, Mintaah dressed gorgeously. She had her hair well-groomed and styled by a beautician and wore an elegant dress to match a pair of well-designed sandals.

She took a Bible and went to notify Showman that she was going to the church. Showman, happy about it, commended her. "Good. You're doing what I've told you." He shook her hand and gave her money. "Take this money for church."

"I appreciate it," Mintaah remarked.

Showman accompanied her out and invoked blessings on her because she was going to church.

Mintaah forced a smiled. "I receive your blessings in good faith. Hope to see you after church."

At church, Mintaah sat in front of the members of the first row where Pastor Essel could easily see her. As Pastor Essel came to stand in the pulpit to preach, she sized him up and thought, *Pastor Essel is a noble man and he can be a good husband to me. He is my choice.*

While Pastor Essel was preaching, he caught sight of Mintaah and realized that she was a newcomer among them so after preaching, he called out the newcomers among them to introduce themselves. "At this point in time, it pleases me to invite the newcomers among us to come forward to introduce themselves."

Mintaah stood up and ambled to the platform. "Today, I'm filled with joy because I'm touched by the pastor's sermon."

"Amen!" Some of the congregation cheered her on. "That is true. Your words are inspirational and superb."

Mintaah, being cheered on, continued her speech. "I'm from Waso, but I've come to stay in this town and I want to worship with you."

"That's good. You're welcome," some of the congregation yelled.

"But before I go to sit down, I'd like to sing a song to glorify God."

"You can sing," some of the congregation yelled.

While Mintaah sang the song, some of the congregation stood up to dance, but Pastor Essel, carried away by the song, waved his right hand above his head amid nodding.

When she finished singing, the secretary of the church approached her to write her name in the attendance register. "You're welcome to worship with us. We, the church leaders, will try to find where you live and visit you at the house."

"I'll be pleased to see you there." Mintaah gave him directions to her house.

At the close of the church service, some of the church members fraternized with her after which Pastor Essel asked her a few questions.

Within a few months, Mintaah had become well known in the church because of her active involvement in most of the church activities. She always went to church early to tidy up the place and arranged the chairs and tables. She also washed the table cloths and curtains of the church windows and doors whenever they were dirty. Such an attitude made Pastor Essel and the leaders and some of the church members admire her.

Having won the admiration of Pastor Essel and most of the church members, she started visiting Pastor Essel and doing household chores, including the washing of utensils, sweeping and ironing of his clothes for him.

Chapter Six

One morning, when Mintaah was ironing Pastor Essel's clothes, he was sitting behind her, a small distance apart and stared at her. *Mintaah is not only well mannered, but also beautiful. She is good material for marriage. Should I marry her?* He thought and called her. "Mintaah, stop the work and come."

Mintaah turned to face him. "Yes pastor." She flipped her hair back and went to sit in a chair which was in front of him.

Pastor Essel looked into her eyes. "When are you going to marry?"

"When God gives me a husband." Mintaah shook her body a little.

"Don't you have any man in mind to marry?"

"No, pastor."

"Okay, you can go."

"Thank you, pastor." Mintaah winked at him.

As Pastor Essel took the Bibles from the table in front of him to the room, Mintaah rushed to collect them. "Pastor, let me take them to the room for you. While Mintaah sauntered towards the room, shaking her buttocks, Pastor Essel followed her. But after she had put the Bibles on a table and was about to come out of the room, she saw a cockroach perching on Pastor Essel's bed.

"Pastor, there's a cockroach on your bed." She pointed out her right hand towards it and took a book to hit it. But it eluded her by flying away to perch on the wall. As she tried to hit it again with the book, it flew away to perch on Pastor Essel's forehead.

"Pastor, hit it. It's perching on your forehead," Mintaah yelled.

But the moment Pastor Essel raised his hand to hit it, it flew away, moving here and there, and while they made attempts to kill it, it perched on Mintaah's left buttock and she stood motionless for Pastor Essel to kill it.

As Pastor Essel stooped down to hit it with a book, it flew away to perch on the bed again and Mintaah took clothes. "This time I won't hit it with a book for it to elude me. I can use these clothes to catch it," she said and stooped down a little and skillfully tossed herself to catch it, but it eluded her by flying away and she fell on the bed and quickly turned to lie supine in the bed. "Why? The cockroach has eluded me again."

"Mintaah, your falling on the bed is strange." Pastor Essel marveled.

"It's unintentional."

While Mintaah lay in the bed, the cockroach flew to perch on her breast, but she remained motionless. "Pastor, come and kill it."

Pastor Essel looked at the cockroach on her breast, moved forward a little and raised the right hand but walked out of the room. "Kill it yourself."

Mintaah quickly hit it. "Pastor, I've killed it. Come and see it." She rushed out of the room to show it to him.

"The cockroach may be a demon. How did you kill it?" Pastor Essel asked.

"I hit it with my hand."

When Mintaah went home, Pastor Essel, who was not pleased with her fall on his bed, pondered, *Did Mintaah intentionally fall on my bed on the pretense of catching the cockroach? Was her attitude a seduction? I've to stop her from coming to do my things for me.* He was in a dilemma. *But why shouldn't I wait to see whether she'll behave like that again to know that her attitude today was a seduction?*

A week after this incident, Showman met with Mintaah. "Has Pastor Essel shown an interest in you by your constant association with him?"

"I've made attempts to make him propose to me, but he is making no effort to do so."

"Don't you think because he is a pastor, he'll let someone propose to you on his behalf to meet their so-called Christian standard?"

"It can be, but if it is so, at least he has to do something directly or indirectly to show he has that intention."

"If he is showing no sign of interest in you, don't be worried. I can still help you to be better off, not through your marriage to a rich man," said Showman, "but through other ways."

"What other ways?" Mintaah asked.

"Some women have become better off through their husbands." Showman stretched out the legs in of front him. "Others too, through their businesses and still others through some secret means."

"What secret means?"

"You'll know it. But are you prepared to do something for me, so that I also help you? The right hand, it is said, washes the left hand and the left hand washes the right hand."

"Why not? I also want to be rich and command prestige and fame like you. Money, regardless of how one gets it, is money."

"Shake my hand. You're thoughtful." Showman was excited.

"Don't be reluctant to tell me any secret that can make me rich." Mintaah pulled at a button of her dress. "I'm prepared to do anything you ask me to do, provided it can make me rich."

Showman took in a sharp breath. "Let's go to the room. The secret of an owl must not be known in the daylight."

Showman put his left hand around Mintaah's neck and they sauntered to the room. "Pastor Essel is a fake pastor and wants to dupe me," he lied.

Mintaah was shocked. "Is Pastor Essel fake? I don't believe it."

"Pastor Essel is my childhood friend as you're aware. What makes him fake is that he and I deal in cocaine. That's why we are close friends," Showman lied.

"Who is to be trusted in this world?" Mintaah marveled. "How can a pastor also be a cocaine dealer?"

"The answer is to amass riches. Let me ask you some questions to prove to you that what I'm saying is not a fabrication. Is Pastor Essel married?"

Mintaah shook the hand. "Not."

"Why is it that a young pastor who is rich has not married?"

"I don't know."

"He knows that when he marries, the wife will get to know his dealings in cocaine and reveal it." Showman's throat wriggled as he spoke. "That's the same reason for which I've divorced my wife who was too inquisitive to know my cocaine dealings."

Mintaah who was shock remarked, "I now know that Pastor Essel is a chameleon in character."

"Exactly and he wants to swindle me of millions of dollars and that million-dollar amount must come to you and me," Showman lied.

"Wow!" The veins in Mintaah's neck jutted out. "Then I'm going to swim in riches."

"That is the reason I've met with you to show you the way." Showman leaned closer to Mintaah. "Pastor Essel will be traveling to Canada in the next three days and on the day before he goes, I want you to secretly put cocaine in his luggage so that he will be accused of being a cocaine dealer and be arrested at the airport if he undergoes security check-ups." He moved his palm over Mintaah's hair to pamper her to agree to his plan. "He has become my enemy and I'll make him have problems and lose respect and fame among people."

Awe transformed Mintaah's face upon hearing the message from Showman. "I can't do this crime? Why should we put a pastor in trouble? What good will we get from putting him in trouble?"

"He has duped me and tarnished my name that I'm a cocaine dealer by preaching about me to people. So, I'll also tarnish his name to teach him a lesson," Showman lied.

"I can't do this task."

"Don't be timid to let money elude you. Don't you want money, something which gives fame and respect? Your success in accomplishing the task will bring you millions of monies."

Mintaah objected to Showman's plan. "I want money but not acquiring it through this way."

"If you want money in genuine ways, then you can't be rich. Most of the rich people we know got their riches through dubious and unscrupulous means." Showman picked up a briefcase and handed it to Mintaah. "If you do the task, you'll have this."

"This bag? For what? What does it contain?" Mintaah asked.

"Open it to see it."

When Mintaah opened it, she was amazed to see bundles of banknotes in cedis, dollars and pound sterling in it. "Do you intend to give me this money on accomplishing the task?"

"Not only this amount. You'll also have a car of your choice and a flight to England where a multi-dollar millionaire has expressed the desire to marry you."

Mintaah smiled. "Are you not flattering me?"

"I mean it. I won't let that fake pastor live to continue to dupe people and be hailed by others."

"I'll do it provided you'll fulfill your promises. If Pastor Essel is fake and he's getting riches, I'll also be fake and get riches."

"That's it. You're now heading towards the path of being rich."

"What will be the evidence that if I do the assignment, you'll fulfill your promises?" Mintaah asked.

"What evidence do you need?"

Mintaah put her palm on her cheek and racked her brain to come up with a plan. "May you swear that you will fulfill your promises if I do the task?"

"To swear is no problem. Let me swear." Showman fetched a cup of water and held it above his head. "Today, I swear by this cup of water that if I don't do my promises upon Mintaah carrying out the said task against Pastor Essel, may severe problems come on me." He poured the water on the floor.

"How do I do the task?" asked Mintaah.

"I'll give you a handful of cocaine in an envelope for you to put in his bag before his travel to Canada."

"All right." Mintaah promised Showman to do the plan.

Chapter Seven

On the day before Pastor Essel set out on the journey to Canada, Mintaah went to do household chores for him. As usual, she swept the house and dusted the furniture in the rooms and washed some cooking utensils in the kitchen. Pastor Essel picked up a pressing iron to iron his clothes for the journey, but Mintaah rushed to collect it. "Pastor, why didn't you call me to iron them for you?"

"I don't want to overburden you with many activities," he said and gave the pressing iron to Mintaah to do the ironing. Pastor Essel sat in a chair and talked with her. "Tomorrow, I'll be traveling to Canada. My colleague pastor has invited me for a program."

"When will you come back?" Mintaah asked.

"I'll spend a week there." Pastor Essel went to the room to take a bag for her. "When you finish ironing the clothes, pack them in the bag," he said and went to the room again.

"Pastor, the bag is beautiful. Is it the one you will use for tomorrow's journey?"

"Yes. This is the bag I use for traveling abroad."

"It's an executive bag." Mintaah collected it, looked inside it and put it down. But the moment Pastor Essel left there for the room, she opened it and took an envelope she had hidden in her dress and put it in one of the pockets in the bag. The envelope contained a handful of cocaine and she packed the clothes in the bag after ironing them.

Pastor Essel didn't see the envelope when he opened the bag and put other things in it. Before he went to bed, he kneeled and held his Bible up to pray. "No weapon that is fashioned against me shall prevail. I refute any tongue that accuses me. I come against any weapon of lies and criminal acts planned against me. Oh God, let my journey to Canada tomorrow be successful in the name of Jesus."

The following day, early in the morning, Pastor Essel set out on the journey to Canada. But before he went to the airport to undergo security check-ups, he sat at a certain place to take a rest. But while he walked majestically, holding his bag, a young man named Kubi who was holding the same type of bag walked after him to spy on him. Kubi was a thief and the servant of Showman, but didn't know that Pastor Essel was Showman's friend. He was going to withdraw money from the bank into the bag for Showman who was also going to Spain that day. While Pastor Essel was resting, Kubi spied on him from a distance. *This man may have money in his bag because he may be a rich man judging from his appearance,* he thought.

Pastor Essel felt the strong urge to urinate so he rushed to find somewhere to urinate, but he forgot to take his bag along. And Kubi, who had already conceived the idea of finding a means to snatch his bag from him, ran to replace his bag with his bag since it was the same as that of Pastor Essel in terms of size, type and color.

When Pastor Essel came back to take his bag, he realized that it was not as heavy as it was, so he opened it only to see that his clothes and other items were not in it. "Somebody has come to steal the things in my bag. What temptation is this? I come against it in the name of Jesus." Being worried, he returned to the house and postponed the journey.

Kubi absconded away to sit somewhere and forcefully opened Pastor Essel's bag and took the money that was in it, without seeing the envelope which contained the cocaine, but he threw away all the clothes and other things in the bag. *If I take these clothes and wear them, I can be caught,* he thought. Being happy that he had got money from Pastor Essel's bag, he rushed to withdraw Showman's money from the bank and put it in the bag purported to be the original bag he was holding and took it to Showman, his master.

"Master, I've brought the money," he said.

"Why have you kept me waiting so long?" Showman asked.

"I had to queue for the money at the bank."

Showman opened the bag and took the money without seeing the envelope which contained the cocaine and counted the money and put it in the bag again. "The money is the correct amount. Take care. When I get to Spain, I'll call you to tell you how things are moving on."

"Yes master," Kubi yelled.

Being in a hurry, Showman set out on the journey to Spain by taking a car to the airport. But at the airport, he had to undergo security check-ups before he took a flight to Spain. During the security check-ups, it was detected that there was cocaine in his bag.

"Sir, you're under arrest. Your bag contains an envelope which contains cocaine," the security personnel explained.

"Where is the envelope?" he asked.

The security personnel showed it to him and he identified it to be the envelope in which he put cocaine and gave to Mintaah to put in Pastor Essel's bag and his face was downcast. "I'm not the person who put the cocaine in my bag."

"Whose bag, is it?" asked the security personnel.

"It's mine," he replied.

"Then you are a cocaine dealer?" The security personnel arrested him and he was dealt with in accordance with the law. They detained him and eventually he was arraigned before the court of law. When all was said and done, the court sentenced him to fifteen years imprisonment. Immediately after the court had given the verdict, the policemen handcuffed him and took him to a prison.

News about this incident spread in many places and the people who knew him were dumbfounded that he was a cocaine dealer. "Not all rich people got their riches through acceptable means and Showman is no exception."

When Mintaah heard Showman's about case, she didn't understand how the envelope of cocaine that she put in Pastor Essel's bag got into Showman's bag leading to his arrest and imprisonment.

When Mintaah realized that Showman's and her plan against Pastor Essel had failed and she wouldn't have what Showman had promised her because he had been imprisoned, she saw the need to continue to seduce Pastor Essel into marrying her so that she would still be better off. *If I seduce Pastor Essel to marry me, I'll be better off and enjoy a good standard of living since he is a well-to-do man. I'll also have a share in his properties and wealth if he becomes my husband. Every woman has the charm to entice a man of her choice into marrying her and I'm going to exercise that charm,* she thought.

With the passage of time, Mintaah devised a means to get Pastor Essel to propose to her, but they were in vain. It seemed he was not noticing her amorous advances towards him. This provoked her and let her make impetuous and risky decisions. *"If Pastor Essel is not going to propose to me despite all my attempts to make him do so, then I will apply unethical and risky methods to seduce him into impregnating me. If I become pregnant by him, he'll quickly perform my marriage rites since he is a pastor and wouldn't like people to notice the pregnancy before he performs my marriage rites.* She had folded her arms in a deep thought.

One day around 4:30 p.m. when Mintaah was performing some chores in the house, Pastor Essel went out of the house to visit his colleague pastor. "Mintaah, I'm going to Pastor Boadu, so don't go home before I come back."

"Yes pastor," Mintaah said, "but when are you coming back?"

"Around 7:00 p.m.," Pastor Essel said and left her.

Mintaah who was now lonely in the house, took a story book to read. After reading for about thirty minutes, she paused and conceived some ideas. *Pastor Essel says he'll come home at 7:00 p.m. and that will be a good time to seduce him. When I see him coming, I'll go and lie in his bed again to seduce him. Even if I fail in this plan, too, he can't tell anyone of it since he is a pastor.*

When it was getting close to 7:00 p.m. Mintaah stood at the entrance of the house to see whether he was coming. As she looked afar, she saw a man coming and she hurried to Pastor Essel's bedroom and opened the door ajar. She undressed herself, leaving on her skimpy underwear and brassiere and lay supine in his bed and opened her legs apart. She closed her eyes and put clothes on her face. *I can't look at Pastor's Essel face while I lie in his bed half naked,* she pondered.

On reaching the entrance of the room, the man was shocked to see the door ajar. *Why? What has happened?* he thought. But the moment he entered the room and saw Mintaah lying half naked in the bed, his heart pounded and he placed a video camera he was holding on a table. He licked his lips and stared at her. *What a set of breasts? Let me go and wake her up. She is asleep,* he thought and sat beside her in the bed and while staring at her, he put his palm on her thigh. "Wake up," he yelled, but Mintaah didn't respond and shook her body and put her left leg on his lap, but he removed it.

Chapter Eight

While Frimpong and Afia were in the room, they embraced each other. Afia sat on Frimpong's lap and kissed him. "You're handsome and can be a replacement of my dead husband. I've cancelled your debt."

"If only my wife will not be a hindrance, I can be a replacement of your dead husband," Frimpong said.

"But for the meantime, you can be my secret husband if not an open one. This will not let your wife know about my relationship with you." Afia held Frimpong's hands.

As Frimpong unbuttoned his shirt, Afia also unzipped her upper garment and hung it on a hanger in the room. But the moment she tried to remove her underwear, she heard a noise outside the room and became suspicious and trembled. "Somebody has come in to house."

"Keep quiet. It's my wife. She has come from the market."

"Then let me wear my dress." The moment Afia took her upper garment and was about to put it on, Frimpong's wife, Araba, banged on the door of the room.

"Sweetheart, open the door. I've come home," she yelled, but Frimpong didn't open it. He made gestures to Afia to hide under the bed and she crawled on her belly to hide there. Frimpong spread a bed sheet on the bed to cover the sides before he opened the door.

"Why did you keep me waiting to open the door?" Araba asked.

"I was sleeping." Frimpong's face wrinkled as he yawned.

When Araba entered the room, she sat in the bed and looked round. "Has Afia come for her money?"

"She came here about two hours ago, but I pleaded with her to give us more time to pay the money."

"What about Munko?"

"He also came here for his money, but I've told him to come tomorrow."

"Why did you tell him to come for it tomorrow?"

"Because he was pestering me to pay it. Don't worry. When he comes tomorrow, I know how I'll talk to him."

Araba saw some dirt on the floor. "The room has not been swept so I want to tidy it up. Dirt might have accumulated under the bed. I'm going for a broom to come and sweep the room."

Afia, who was hiding under the bed, heard her statement and became afraid that she would be caught if she swept the room. *Is Frimpong's wife coming to sweep the room? Then she'll see me and disgrace will befall me. Today, I'm doomed,* she thought.

As soon as Araba walked out of the room for a broom to sweep the room, Frimpong grabbed her hand. "Wait. Don't sweep the room now. I'm hungry and you must prepare some food for me."

"How many minutes will it take to sweep the room? Let me sweep the room first." She ambled away for a broom in another room, but since she was not finding it, she had to search for it and thus, it delayed her coming back to the bedroom.

During this period, Frimpong told Afia, who was hiding under the bed, to come out of the room and he asked her to hide in an empty barrel which they used to store water.

Since Araba was unable to find the broom, she came back to Frimpong. "I can't find the broom. Have you seen it anywhere?"

"No. But have you searched for it properly in the room?"

"Yes." She nodded. "Let me postpone the sweeping and prepare some food for you since you're hungry." She strolled along the corridor to take a bucket.

"What's the bucket for?" Frimpong asked.

"I want to fetch water into the barrel because I'll need water to prepare the food and there is no water in it."

Frimpong held her hands to pull her towards him. "Why don't you let me fetch the water into the barrel while you slice the vegetables?"

Araba eluded him and rushed for a bucket. "Fetching water into the barrel has not been your duty. It's my duty."

"But today, I want to do it to exercise my body."

Afia, hiding in the barrel, shivered uncontrollably and her jaws moved up and down. *"Is Frimpong's wife coming to fetch water into this barrel? How can I explain my being in the barrel, holding my upper garment, if she sees me?"* she pondered.

Araba turned on the tap which pumped water into the bucket and as she strolled along the corridor to pour the water into the barrel, Frimpong rushed to stand in front of the barrel. "My precious wife, let me help you pour the water into the barrel because the bucket is heavy to lift." He got hold of the bucket and she handed it to him and he poured the water into the barrel while Afia was squatting in it. He blinked the eyes to signal to her not to talk or do something that would make Araba see her.

"One more, "he said and gave the bucket to Araba." I'm standing here. Fetch the water to me while I also pour it into the barrel."

But when Araba had fetched the water for the second time, she insisted that she pour it into the barrel, but Frimpong resisted her. He argued with her and got hold of the bucket and forcefully snatched it from her hand, but it slipped from his hand and the water in it spilled over the floor.

"Why didn't you let me pour the water into the barrel?" Frimpong frowned. "Go and bring me the mop to mop the water on the floor."

Araba hurried to the room to pick up the mop to mop the water, but Frimpong snatched it from her. "Let me mop it. Go to the market to buy me some food instead of cooking it."

"Sweetheart, why are you stopping me from cooking the food for you? Are you angry at me?" Araba wife asked.

"I'm hungry and cooking the food for me will be a delay."

Being convinced of Frimpong's explanation, she hurried to the room to take a basket and dashed to the market to buy some food for him. The moment she left the house for the market, Frimpong heaved a sigh. "I'm lucky that my wife didn't see Afia in the barrel."

Without delay, he let Afia come out from the barrel and she wore her wet upper garment, which she was holding in the barrel and absconded away.

Chapter Nine

As the man removed Mintaah's leg on his lap, she wriggled her body in the bed and put her palm on his chest to caress it, and he didn't show any resistance. He also caressed her and eventually they did the unthinkable; they had sex. While making love, Mintaah explained, "I can't look at your face while we're sinning. If I look at your face, it will remind me of the Bible and make me have a guilty conscious."

But unknown to Mintaah, the person whom she had seduced and was making love with was not Pastor Essel, but his twin brother, Bentil, who was the exact resemblance of Pastor Essel and had come to the room and being carried away by lust made love with her. His physical features such as the height, stature, complexion, and every part of him were the same as that of Pastor Essel, so Mintaah mistook him to be Pastor Essel. Indeed,

Bentil was a mistaken identity. But Mintaah didn't know he was Pastor Essel's twin and she went home thinking that she had succeeded in seducing Pastor Essel.

Since Bentil was mentally ill and needed much care and medical attention, he was staying with his sister in a faraway town for her to take care of him.

When Mintaah had gone home after making love with Bentil, Pastor Essel came to meet Bentil in the room.

"How? I can see you're much better," Pastor Essel remarked.

"Yes brother. My doctor is good. He often comes to check on me," said Bentil.

"Have you finished taking the full course of the drugs the doctor prescribed for you last month?"

"Yes. And I'm here for money for another course of drugs he wants me to buy."

"But didn't you come to see a young woman here?"

"I came to meet her, but she has gone home since I'm here. She explained that it was getting late."

The next day, early in the morning, Pastor Essel gave Bentil, his twin brother, money and saw him off. "Send my greetings to our sister for me."

A month later, Mintaah didn't have her menstrual cycle and she showed signs and symptoms of being pregnant. She went for a medical check-up and after the doctor had carried out a series of tests on her, he confirmed that she was pregnant. "Mintaah, the test indicates that you're pregnant."

"Doctor, that's good news to me."

The doctor gave her some vitamins to take. "Eat well and take these vitamins."

"I'll do that." She collected the pills and went home. She rushed to Pastor Essel to notify him of the pregnancy.

"Pastor, I'm here to tell you some news," she said, oozing with enthusiasm.

"Is it good news?" asked Pastor Essel.

"Of course."

"Then I'm all ears."

"Pastor, I'm now carrying your seed in my womb."

"My seed in your womb? What does it mean?" Pastor Essel rocked back and forth in his chair.

Mintaah looked intently into his face. "Pastor, I'm preg-, preg-, nant."

"What? Pregnant? Why did you become pregnant before you have married? Are you not aware that God detests pregnancy before marriage?"

"I know, but it is a mistake. However, we can put things right since God is merciful to forgive us our sins."

"Have you notified the person who is responsible for it?"

"That's why I'm here to do so."

"Is the person a member of the church that you want me to know about?"

"Yes, pastor."

Pastor Essel was curious. "Who is the person?"

Mintaah lowered her head to look downwards. "Pastor, you're responsible."

"What? Me? Pastor Essel stood up in astonishment. "Are you making a mockery of yourself?"

"I'm serious, pastor."

"Mintaah, are you losing your mind that you're talking like that?"

Mintaah raised her head to look at him. "Have you forgotten what we did last month?"

"What did we do last month?"

"Pastor, I expect you to remember. Don't you remember what you did to me in your bedroom last month?" Mintaah muttered.

"Mintaah, are you dreaming or hallucinating?" Pastor Essel sat up.

"I'm not dreaming or hallucinating. What I'm saying is the truth." Mintaah twirled her hair. "The baby in my womb is the product of what you did to me in your bedroom last month." She didn't mince words.

"What temptation is this? God, save me from this problem." Pastor Essel held Mintaah's hands and looked into her eyes. "Mintaah, do you want to put my integrity as a pastor into disrepute and disgrace me?"

"That's the reason you shouldn't delay performing my marriage rites before the pregnancy becomes visible and known to people." Mintaah rolled her eyes as she spoke in a soft voice. "I haven't disclosed it to anyone and I suggest you perform my marriage rites to my relatives with all alacrity."

Pastor Essel rose from his seat and stood akimbo. "Mintaah, why do you want to wrongly accuse me of the pregnancy?" He grabbed her and shook her. "You're my enemy in disguise and a scoundrel who wants to slander me. Leave my house."

"To force me from your house means you're forcing your baby in my womb from your house. Is this good? You must be a practical pastor and act that way."

Day in, and day out, Mintaah pestered Pastor Essel with the need to accept the pregnancy, but he refused. "How can I accept a pregnancy from a woman who is not my wife and whom I haven't had any sexual affair with? The word of God does not enjoin me to do that."

"Pastor, to tell me this is to be sanctimonious. How can you deny having a sexual affair with me? Have you forgotten the day you had a feel of my body?" Mintaah rocked on her feet as she burned with anger. "Do you want me to let people know about it before you accept it? Why don't you perform my marriage rites early to protect your integrity as a pastor from being ruined?"

Pastor Essel scrunched up his face and raised the voice. "I'm not responsible for the pregnancy and you can do whatever you like. I don't care."

When all Mintaah's attempts to make Pastor Essel accept the pregnancy had proved futile, she discussed the issue with the leaders of the church. Without hesitation, the elders summoned Pastor Essel and put the issue before him.

"Pastor Essel, Mintaah says you're responsible for her pregnancy. Is it true?" one of the elders asked.

"No."

"Mintaah, are you sure Pastor Essel is responsible for the pregnancy?" asked the elder.

"Yes. How can I mention Pastor Essel for being responsible for my pregnancy if he is not the one? No woman would do that."

"Pastor Essel, there have been rumors everywhere in this town that Mintaah always comes to your home to do household chores for you. Is it true?" asked one of the other elders.

"Yes."

"Don't you think such a situation could fuel a sexual relationship between you two?"

"It could, but it hasn't happened in my case."

"Pastor Essel, do you think Mintaah would say you have impregnated her while it's not true?"

"I don't expect her to say that. Nevertheless, she has said it."

The senior pastor cleared his throat." Pastor Essel, will it be wrong if we believe what Mintaah is saying by the fact that she always comes to your house to do household chores for you?"

"It's true that Mintaah always comes to do household chores for me, but it's not true that I've impregnated her." He pulled a handkerchief from his pocket to mop his face.

After a series of discussions, questions and answers, the elders of the church suspended Pastor Essel from his pastoral office while investigations were being carried out.

"Pastor Essel, following Mintaah's claim that you've impregnated her, we, the elders of the church, have unanimously agreed in accordance with the church rules that you should not be in the pastoral office for the meantime.

"By this, from today, you're not to stand in the pulpit to preach and offer the Lord's Supper. Until further notice, you're no longer a pastor of the church and you can't perform any pastoral duties in the church. However, the church reserves the right to restore you to your pastoral office if our investigations proves you innocent."

Pastor Essel, whose face was downcast, looked into heaven and muttered, "Vindication comes from God."

News circulated everywhere that Pastor Essel had impregnated one of his church members and had denied the pregnancy. Some radio and television stations discussed it and many people who heard the news could not believe their ears and some of them castigated him.

"Pastor Essel is not a man of God. He has impregnated a woman in his church and denied the pregnancy. It is only a fake pastor who would do this," a girl remarked.

"The so-called Pastor Essel should be made to face the full rigors of the law because it is not right to impregnate a woman and deny the pregnancy. Who should take care of the baby?" an old man said, jeering at him.

Despite the castigations and the assortment of insults heaped on Pastor Essel, he didn't waver in his Christian faith. He continued to pray fervently and studied the word of God to increase his faith to make him immune to criticisms. "The word of God in Isaiah 54:17 makes me understand that no weapon that is fashioned against me shall prevail, I'll refute every tongue that accuses me and my vindication comes from God," he said whenever he prayed.

Six months after Mintaah had mentioned him for being responsible for her pregnancy, the leaders of the church held another meeting with them.

"Pastor Essel and Mintaah, it has become necessary to have this meeting with you to resolve and finalize the issue at stake," the church leaders said.

"Pastor Essel, what do you have to say about Mintaah's claim that you're responsible for her pregnancy?"

"How can I accept a pregnancy from a woman whom I haven't had any sexual affair with?"

Mintaah stood up in haste. "He is lying. He is my bedfellow and the result of it is the pregnancy."

Ton of the leaders wondered at Mintaah's statement. "Why should a pastor be a bedfellow of a woman who is not his wife? Is it not for a sexual purpose that a pastor will do so?"

While the discussion was going on amid arguments and misunderstandings between Pastor Essel and Mintaah, Bentil, Pastor Essel's twin brother, whom Mintaah mistakenly seduced, came in. All eyes were fixed on him and he started shouting, "I'm looking for my brother, Pastor Essel." But the secretary of the church ordered him to stop shouting. "Keep quiet. We're having a meeting here."

Bentil giggled, moving forth and back.

Pastor Essel talked to him and asked him to sit in a chair and wait for him. "I'm having a meeting. Sit on this chair to wait for me," he told Bentil.

As Bentil looked at the people gathered there, he saw Mintaah and remembered that she was the one whom he had sex with. So, he hurried to squat before her and looked at her face and laughed. "May I kiss you?" He forcefully grabbed Mintaah's head with both hands and put his lips on hers to kiss her.

The church leaders, who were shocked at Bentil's attitude, rushed to separate Mintaah from his grip. "Stop doing this. Do you want to seduce her in our sight?" they remarked.

"Don't stop me. She is my girlfriend and bedfellow."

"Pastor Essel, talk to your twin brother to stop misbehaving at this meeting," the church leaders mumbled.

"Don't be surprised at his actions. He is not of a sound mind."

Bentil jumped while laughing. "No one can stop me from expressing love to my girlfriend."

Mintaah spat and stamped on the floor. "Don't say that again. I'm your brother's prospective wife."

"Hahaha!" Bentil swung the right leg in the air. "Come and see that you're my girlfriend and bedfellow."

"See what?" Mintaah yelled.

"Mintaah, don't mind my brother. He is mentally ill," Pastor Essel said.

Bentil was still rowdy and opened his mouth wide and belched. "Pastors, come and see that Mintaah is my girlfriend and bedfellow and I've the right to kiss her."

"Shut up. Stop your madness," the church secretary shouted.

"Come and see." Bentil switched on his video camera and showed it to them. "See that this woman is my girlfriend and bedfellow and I've the right to kiss her anywhere."

To the surprise of the people gathered there, the video camera showed Bentil and Mintaah making love in Pastor Essel's bedroom. It showed Mintaah lying half naked in the bed and had covered her face with clothes while Bentil was making love with her. The video camera showed that whenever Bentil tried to remove the clothes covering Mintaah's face, she would close her eyes, saying, "Pastor I can't look at your face while we are sinning. If I see your face, it will remind me of the Bible."

On seeing the video, all the people, including the pastor, were swallowed up in astonishment and believed that Pastor Essel was not responsible for Mintaah's pregnancy and that it was a calculated attempt of Mintaah to seduce him into impregnating her for him to marry her.

When Mintaah saw the video and realized that the person whom she had seduced into impregnating her was not Pastor Essel, but his twin brother who was mentally ill, she was crippled with shock and collapsed and some men took her to a hospital. On gaining consciousness, she confessed that she wanted to seduce Pastor Essel into impregnating her so that she would get married to him. She also confessed how Showman influenced her to put cocaine into his bag but the plan backfired.

Within a few days, information had spread in the town that Mintaah had seduced Bentil, a mentally ill person, into impregnating her.

"The unthinkable has happened. Someone who is mentally ill has been able to impregnate Mintaah. Mintaah has seduced the wrong person into impregnating her. This attests to the fact that if you plan evil for a man of God, evil befalls you," some people said.

Furthermore, journalists and media men who investigated the case reported it in newspapers, and on the radio and television. Consequently, Mintaah became an object of ridicule and the topic of discussion in many places.

As people hurled insults and insinuations at her, she left the town to live in Sundo to avoid further embarrassments and disgrace. During the eight month of the pregnancy, she had some complications and bled profusely which resulted in her death.

Fiction Books By Isaac Nkrumah Darko

- **Pregnant Husband**

- **Mistaken Love**

- **Abandoned Child**

- **The Evil Plan**

- **Married To A Snake**

- **The Deception**